This Walker book belongs to:

_____

_____

_____

For our mums and our dads, who always
made sure we were nourished and well fed
D. H. & S. S.

First published 2015 by Walker Books Ltd
87 Vauxhall Walk, London SE11 5HJ

This edition published 2016

2 4 6 8 10 9 7 5 3 1

© 2015 Dean Hacohen and Sherry Scharschmidt

The right of Dean Hacohen and Sherry Scharschmidt to be identified as author/
illustrators of this work has been asserted by them in accordance with the Copyright,
Designs and Patents Act 1988

This book has been typeset in Journal and Providence Sans

Printed in China

British Library Cataloguing in Publication Data:
a catalogue record for this book is available from the British Library

ISBN 978-1-4063-6578-8

www.walker.co.uk

Who's Hungry?

Dean Hacohen &
Sherry Scharschmidt

WALKER BOOKS
AND SUBSIDIARIES
LONDON · BOSTON · SYDNEY · AUCKLAND

Time to eat.

Who's hungry?

I am! I'm hungry!

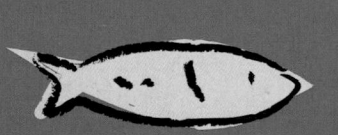

I am! I would love
a fresh fish, please.

You're quick, Seal!
Who else is hungry?

I am! Bananas are
my favourite.

You're welcome, Monkey.
Who else is hungry?

I am!
I like hay.

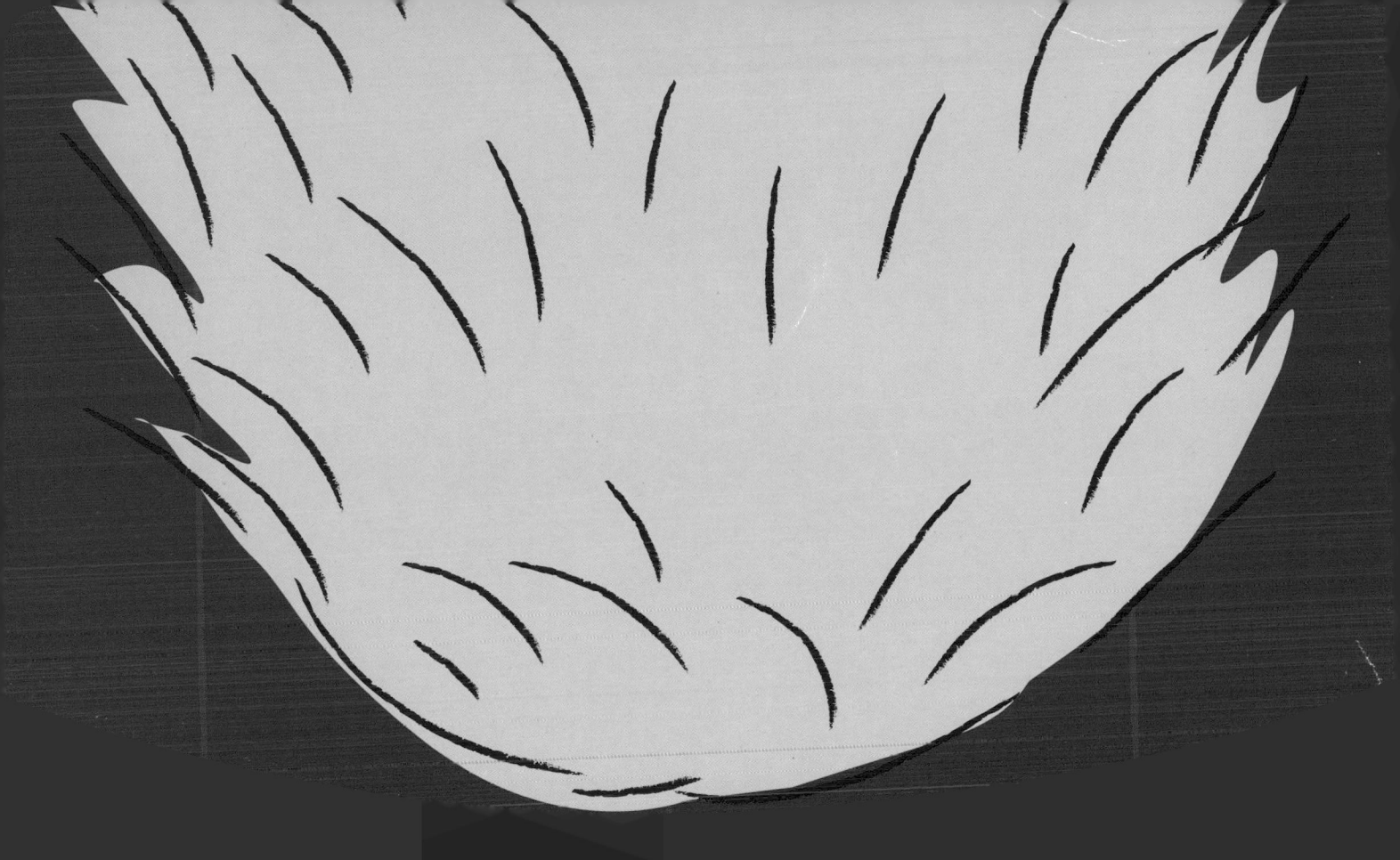

What a big appetite, Horse!
Who else is hungry?

I am! I would like
an acorn, please.

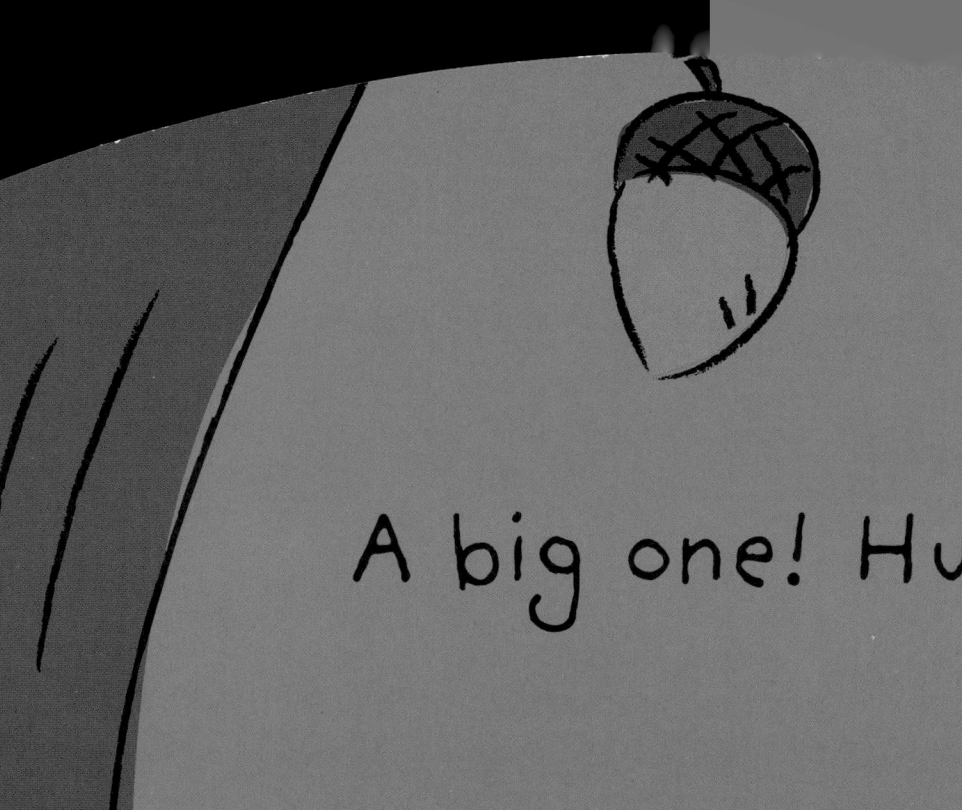

A big one! Hurray!

It's all yours, Squirrel.
Who else is hungry?

I am! I can't wait
to chew some bamboo.

There's plenty more, Panda!
Who else is hungry?

I am! Please may I have some cheese?

So tasty!

Enjoy it, Mouse!
Is anyone else hungry?

Are you hungry?
Eat up!

Enjoyed feeding the animals?

Now get the baby animals ready for bed in *Tuck Me In!* – the bestselling companion title to *Who's Hungry?*

ISBN 978-1-4063-3203-2

Available from all good booksellers

www.walker.co.uk